MW00954070

This book is dedicated to our beautiful Nanna D.
She is our shining light and missed dearly every day.

Authors: Sarah Cullen & Carmen Ellis
Artwork & Book Design © Zuzana Svobodová

Title: Stella, The Shark Who Loves Treasure

ISBN 978-0-6453650-5-4 (Paperback)
ISBN 978-0-6453650-4-7 (Hardcover)
ISBN 978-0-6453650-3-0 (eBook)

the SHARK who LOVES TREASURE

STELLA

written by
Sarah Cullen
Carmen Ellis

illustrated by
Zuzana
Svobodová

Stella the shark lived alone in her lair.
While most were quite gloomy, her lair had some flare.
The whole place was shining with colors so bright
for trinkets and treasures were Stella's delight.

From diamonds to moonstones, this shark loved them all.
No sapphire's too big and no opal too small.
No matter how large her collection became,
there was still one more trinket she needed to claim...

"The 'Rose of the Sea,'" bright, shiny, and red,
the perfect addition to hang 'round her head.

That will be the last piece, Stella thought with a grin.
I can't wait to hold it at last in my fin.
There's a rumor it lies at the floor of the sea
in an old sunken ship in a chest with a key.

She knew of a friend who could help find the chest–
an orca named Rory who loved a good quest.

Once she had found him, she told him her story.
"I know how to find that old ship!" exclaimed Rory.
"When you get to the cave you swim all the way through,
you'll soon find that ship, but I'm coming with you!"

The shark and the orca set out on their way,
but Stella stopped briefly, just so she could say,
"When we find the red rose in the depths of the sea,
just try to remember, the treasure's for me."

They found the old ship that lay wrecked on the floor,
and the key for the chest
had been hung near a door.

When trying to squeeze through a hole on the side,
poor Stella got stuck. "I CAN'T REACH IT," she cried.

She squeezed
and she wriggled
with all of her
might,

but Stella was round,
and the hole was
quite tight.

Huffing and puffing, her face turning blue,
she plummeted backwards. "Now what do we do?"

Rory said, "Hold it! Let me have a try!
Maybe I can break through. I'm a big burly guy."
He lifted his tail and then gave a huge whack,
but he just bounced right off without making a crack.

"We need to sit down and to have a quick break
to work out a different angle to take."
"No problem," said Stella. "But still understand,
when we find the treasure, it's mine as we've planned."

Rory suggested
the help of a friend.
"I know of a guy that
can twist and can bend.

An octopus surely
could pick up the key
that opens the chest
where the treasure must be."

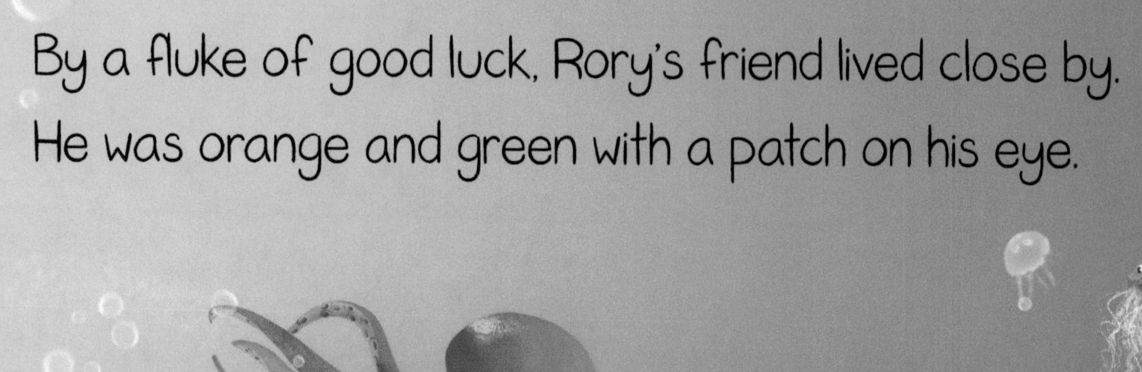

By a fluke of good luck, Rory's friend lived close by.
He was orange and green with a patch on his eye.

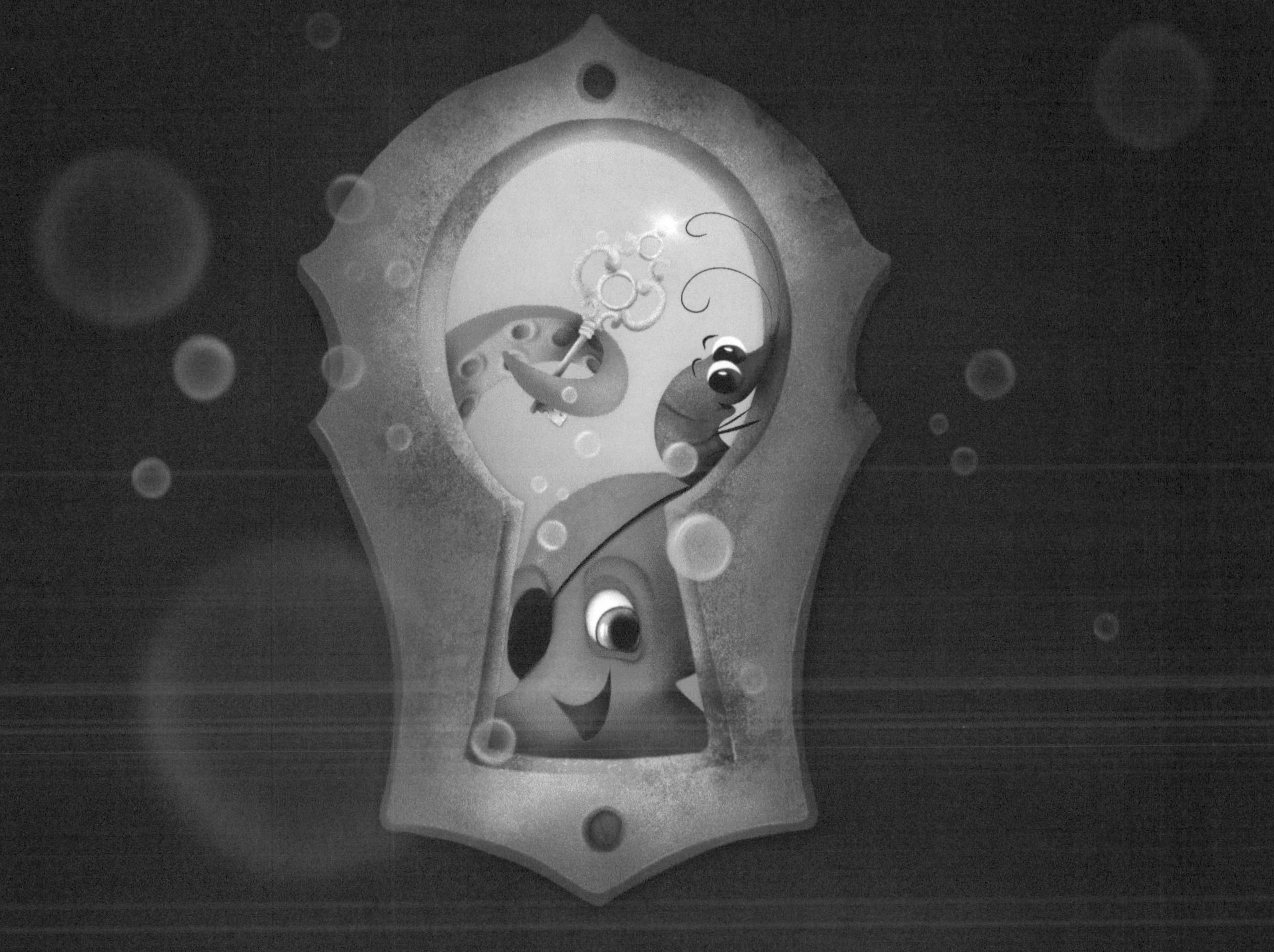

With a smile on his face, Otto reached his arm through.
"I'll pick up the key and I'll open it too!"
"That's great!" replied Stella. "I'm sure you'll do fine,
but don't you forget that the treasure is mine."

He turned the key once, and the chest opened wide.
"The 'Rose of the Sea' is all mine!" Stella cried.

The rose had three rubies,
so shiny and bright,
but something about
this just didn't feel right.

Would it feel better to give them away?
They could each have one stone.
It would brighten their day.

From that moment on,
she decided to share and
gathered the treasures
that filled up her lair.

"I'll pass these around.
They're no longer just mine.
Now the whole ocean
can shimmer and shine!"

Fun facts

1. What does a shark's skin feel like?

A) Rough

B) Smooth

C) Slimy

2. Sharks are older than dinosaurs.

A) True

B) False

3. Which shark is the biggest?

A) Great white shark

B) Basking shark

C) Whale shark

4. Do sharks have any bones in their body?

A) Yes

B) No

5. How many hearts does an octopus have?

A) 1

B) 2

C) 3

Answers

1. A) A shark's skin is rough like sandpaper.
2. A) True, sharks have been around for more than 420 million years.
3. C) The whale shark is the biggest, followed by the basking shark
4. B) No, sharks don't have bones in their body. They have a skeleton that is made from cartilage.
5. C) An octopus has 3 hearts.

Hi there, Carmen and Sarah here. We are sisters from NSW, Australia. Together, we share a love of the ocean and all the beautiful creatures in it. Through these books, we would love to encourage children from all over the world to share their ***passion of the ocean*** and protect it for years to come. We welcome you to join us on Instagram and Facebook where you can see sneak peaks of future projects, learn more about the ocean and even help to choose names of characters and other decisions in the book making process.

These books would not be possible without our beautiful illustrator Zuzana Svobodová. If you want to follow Zuzana and see more of her ***stunning illustrations***, her Instagram is @zuzana_svobodova_illustration.

We cannot thank you enough for your support. Without you we would not be able to keep making our beloved Ocean Tales. If you would like to help keep our dream alive, an honest review on Amazon would help us to spread the word.

Much love from our families to yours.

www.instagram.com/oceantaleschildrensbooks

www.facebook.com/Ocean-Tales-Childrens-Books-100332601636543

www.oceantaleschildrensbooks.com.a

CPSIA information can be obtained
at www.ICGtesting.com
Printed in the USA
LVHW070344180723
752690LV00007B/153